MW00412911

Secrets, Lies, & Murder

Case #664

Journal of Hudson Blackwell

Published by Cursed Pen Publishing
in association with Murder Mystery Box

www.cursedpen.com
Caretaker@murdermysterybox, MurderMysteryBox.com

Copyright © 2016 by Hudson Blackwell. All rights reserved.

In accordance with the U.S. Copyright Act of 1976, the uploading,
scanning, emailing, and electronic sharing or reproduction of any part of
this book without written permission of the publisher constitutes illegal
piracy and theft of the author's intellectual property. If one would like to
use material from this book (other than review purposes), prior permission
must be attained by contacting the publisher at pr@cursedpen.com.

Thank you for your support of the author's rights.

ISBN   978-1530710263

Title Page art work by Cursed Pen © 2016 Cursed Pen

This is a work of fiction. Names, characters, locations and incidents either
are the product of the author's imagination or are used fictitiously, and any
resemblance to actual persons, living or dead, businesses, companies, events
or locales is entirely coincidental

Dedicated to a hell of a woman,

my best friend,

my mother,

Rene'

Travel day over! Man, oh man!

I feel like I'm still on that plane. The flight wasn't long, but there was a screaming toddler on the flight that made it feel four times as long, I swear. At last I'm here, though on Hawaii's big island. It's been so long since I've seen my brother, I hardly recognized him when I saw him at the airport. Marc wore his butler attire and gave me the royal treatment. He even brought the town car to pick me up. He's real good at his job, and I'm proud of my little brother. He's happy, and that's everything in life.

We arrived at the Waterworth estate at sunset, and it's more beautiful than I remembered.

We followed a private driveway with vibrant trees and plants, like nothing the mainland can grow.

These stunning colors are only present in this place,
I'm sure of it. The house is mammoth with columns
outside the front door, engraved with intricate
designs. It's been a while since I've been inside the
Waterworth House, but last I recall, it's like a museum
in that place.

The service staff's quarters are tucked off
the side of the residence. There are separate
apartments contained within a single building for the
butler (Marc) and the chef. Each unit is a quaint two
bedroom, one bathroom apartment complete with
laundry and storage rooms.

Marc showed me to the guest room in his
apartment. It's decorated exactly as it was the last
time I stayed here. That had to be, what? Five years
ago? Yeah, it's been a while.

Across from the bedroom door is a full-sized
bed with a blue, hibiscus-patterned bedding set.
There's even a bed skirt. White curtains cover the

windows across from the door and on the adjacent wall. A bamboo, four-drawer dresser is along the entry wall, with matching nightstands on either side of the bed. Pieces of abstract art Chef Holloway painted years ago hang on the walls.

This place is comfortable. Familiar.

Just being here, I already feel all the stresses of real life floating away. It's like the Hawaiian waves grab hold of my troubles and take them out with the tide. Those waves can keep 'em.

What I need is time to evaluate my life. That's why I'm here. Things just aren't that good back home. I mean, I make a decent pay as a private investigator, I'm not complaining. It's just, the job is all I have. I have two ex-wives and my kids are grown now. They don't want anything to do with me. I think I need to change course a little bit. I'm hoping this time of relaxation will help me gain a little perspective.

Oh, I almost forgot!

When we arrived, Mrs. Waterworth insisted Marc and I join the family for dinner tonight. Apparently, the Waterworth's are having a family reunion this week. Mrs. Waterworth promised not to cut into my vacation, as long as I join the family for dinner. How could I refuse?

Dinner with the Waterworth's was rather entertaining. Everything was set up buffet style.

The spread was divine. At the head of the buffet table was a marmalade-glazed, roast turkey and a brown sugar glazed ham, followed by garlic mashed potatoes, roasted asparagus, a tossed spinach salad and so much more. Chef Holloway really out did himself.

The food was the best I've had in a long, long time, but it paled in comparison to the company.

Mrs. Waterworth (she insisted that I call her Poppy) is just a tiny little thing. She can't be more than 5' 1" —or so, but she sure is a spit-fire. Quick witted and hilarious! She could be a stand-up comedian. I so enjoyed her company. I couldn't imagine a more welcoming host.

Her husband, Mel, indulged a little too much bourbon, but it only made him more approachable. He's a great-big, hulking man, so I imagine it must have taken a great deal of bourbon. He danced with his wife and looked to be having a terrific time. Both Mel and Poppy were dressed in the finest.

Apparently, Poppy hasn't had her family all together since she moved to Hawaii eleven years ago. She seems happy to have them all in her house, but I get the distinct feeling they aren't as happy to be here.

Mel and Poppy's son, Angel seemed bored for the entire night. He's a curious looking young man. He was dressed in all black, with black nail polish on his nails—which he'd been chewing on for half the night. His dark, shaggy hair and appearance screamed punk rock for some reason. Kids these days... The thing is, he's not really a kid. I think he's eighteen or nineteen.

At Angel's side all night, was his cousin and nephew to Poppy, Randall. He didn't talk much to anyone but Angel. Randall's about the same age and is a little taller than Angel, but far more clean cut. He had dark circles beneath his eyes, which makes me think he's been having trouble sleeping.

Randall's mother, Rose, who is Poppy's sister, is a stunner. Her long, blond hair and even longer legs are a sight. She went on and on about the Waterworth's belongings, complementing everything. I have a feeling that her compliments weren't meant as kindness. Man, that woman is beautiful, but I think her outward beauty is far more appealing than her inward beauty.

Betty, Poppy's cousin wore a little black dress to dinner. And by little, I mean tiny. She looked like a seductress on the prowl with her black stilettos. She pawed at everyone when she talked to them. The strange thing is, nearly all the attendees were her family.

Poppy's brother, Lyle was short with everyone except Rose and Betty. He's a tall, lanky man with short, black hair, graying at the sides. He has a slight salt and pepper stubble and worry lines around his eyes and on his forehead.

I overheard Betty chatting with Lyle. She said the only reason she came was because Poppy paid for the round trip flight to Hawaii. She wanted to ask Poppy for some money. To which Lyle replied, "Good luck with that. Poppy has a death grip on her money. You'd think she was dirt poor the way that scrooge clutches to every last penny."

It caught me a little off guard to hear Poppy's brother speak poorly of her. Personally, I think it was rather generous of her to invite Marc and me to their family dinner. Plus, she paid for their travel here. Eh, but that's family, right? Everyone's got something to complain about.

Tomorrow, I have a beach day planned at the black sand beach. I can let these calloused feet of mine get a little exfoliating in the coarse sand and cool waters. Maybe see some sea turtles or check out some ladies in skimpy bikinis...

This vacation was such a good idea.

I don't know where to begin this entry. So much has happened. I think I'll take it one step at a time and start at the beginning. Several conversations took place, so I am going to dictate them in this journal. This way I can review them later for consistency.

About an hour ago, I woke up after hearing a scream from the main house. It was followed by another. I looked out my window and could see lights illuminating in various windows. Apparently, I wasn't the only one wakened this way. I hurried to my brother's door. He didn't answer, but he's always been a heavy sleeper. I opened the door and there he was sprawled out on the bed like when he was a teenager. I called out to him. He lifted his head with one eye squinted.

"Screams are coming from the house," I told him.

"The Waterworth house?" Marc asked.

I nodded.

He leapt to his feet and pulled on his uniform, a tux, in record time. He even made sure to put on a fresh pair of white gloves. Marc definitely takes his job seriously.

I pulled on my twill trousers and slung on my sports jacket over a cotton tee. Marc made me feel self-conscience by getting all snazzed up.

We jogged to the main house. Marc took the lead. He opened the side door to the kitchen with a key from his pocket. I followed him through the service staff entrance and locked it behind me, per his instruction.

We passed through the kitchen and followed the echoes of voices in the distance. I could hear sobbing amongst the voices. We followed a short hallway and turned a corner. As Marc and I made the turn, we could see what all the commotion was about. At the end of the long hallway, in front of a door, the family gathered around. Suspended above them was the body of Poppy Waterworth. A step stool lay on its side beneath her body. I felt as though someone had suddenly plunged a knife through my stomach. The air left my lungs in seeing the light extinguished from our gracious host. Poppy Waterworth had committed suicide.

Marc and I stood in the hallway between the library and one of the guest rooms. When Mel spotted Marc, he rushed to my brother and begged him to phone the police.

"We can't leave her up there," Mel said, cupping his hands over his mouth.

"You can't touch anything until the police get here," Lyle said.

"Don't you start with me!" Mel shouted. "That is my wife up there!"

I placed my hand on Mel's shoulder.

"Mr. Waterworth, I'm afraid the police are going to need everything to remain untouched until they process it. Marc is phoning the police right now. Come, let's go into the library. You shouldn't see her like this. In fact, no one should. We should all get out of the hallway."

Mel looked at me, as tears slid down his cheeks, and nodded.

"Everyone, into the library," he ordered.

They all followed us into the room. I helped Mel to a leather chair near the fireplace.

I tried to collect my thoughts. I hadn't expected this, not at all. This evening Poppy didn't seem like the type of woman who would take her own life. Then again, I'd only really socialized with her this evening. On my other visits to Hawaii, the

Waterworth family had been gone, on vacations of their own. I didn't know her well enough to say for certain what her state of mind was at the time of the suicide.

Marc returned and announced the police were on the way. Tears snuck down the corners of Marc's eyes. He turned away in an attempt to regain his composure. I went to him and patted his shoulder. Staring out at the books on the shelf in front of us, I left my hand in place. I wish I had the right words to console my brother in that moment. He's worked for Mrs. Waterworth for eleven years. She hired him a few weeks after moving to Hawaii. He cares about this family as if they are an extended part of his. And yet, he feels the need to hide his emotions from them. Marc...always the professional.

I simply cannot understand why this woman would do such a thing.

We all waited for the police and it didn't take them long to arrive. The officers took all of our statements, one by one. They asked me general questions, nothing evasive. Questions like:

"Did Mrs. Waterworth seem upset or depressed? Did she seem like someone who would take her own life?"

After both Marc and I had given our statements, he pulled me to the kitchen for a quick conversation.

"She didn't kill herself," Marc whispered.

I asked, "What do you mean?"

I felt a little shocked.

"I know Poppy. She would never do something like this. I know it. There has to be more to this than what it looks like. She was too strong willed to do this. Mrs. Waterworth would have never given up on life. Other than her money grubbing family, her life was well. She didn't do this."

"Okay Marc, if Mrs. Waterworth didn't hang herself in the hallway, someone else did. That would mean someone killed her."

Marc took a deep breath and glanced around. "I know," he whispered

"Did you tell the police?"

"I told them she didn't seem the type to do something like this and left it at that. Hudson, I know this is your vacation, but will you please look into her death? I think there is more to this and I trust you more than anyone."

"Of course. I know she was like family. I'm sorry for your loss."

So it seems, even on my vacation, I've been roped into a case. Marc and I only just returned from the main house to try to catch a little sleep, but I don't think either of us will. How can a person catch forty winks after all that's happened? Once the sun comes up, I'll begin my investigation. I think I'll start with a few conversations with the family, to see where it'll go. I'll follow up later at the police station. It's likely the police won't be forthright with me, but at least I can try.

My mind has been running all night. I haven't gone back to sleep. The more I think about things, the more I think Marc might be right. I have a feeling Poppy Waterworth didn't hang herself... It means someone in that house is a killer.

I was able to snap a few pictures of the scene without making it look obvious. The last thing I want to do is make the family feel that I may be insensitive to the situation. It's quite the opposite. I noticed beside the stool, were two peculiar things:

A typed suicide note signed by Poppy

A post card sent to Betty (Poppy's cousin) inviting her to the reunion.

Why? Why would someone kill her? There is the obvious, money. She was loaded. I need to talk more to the family to see if I can uncover any motivations.

[OPEN EVIDENCE ENVELOPE #1]

I met with Mel Waterworth this morning. He is distraught about the loss of his wife. It could all be an act; I don't know him well enough to tell for certain. Last night, I recall him refilling his bourbon glass several times. Near the night's end he was stumbling around and Poppy helped him to bed. She'd returned fine and continued entertaining. I had a feeling this was not the first time she'd done that for him. Still, she didn't seem upset about it. He wasn't out of hand, just having a good time, until he started losing his balance.

I met Mel on the front porch of the house. The view is magnificent. The sprawling lawn goes on and on, enveloped by Palm and Banyan trees stretching toward the clear sky. Marc brought Mel and I organic black tea.

It felt too weird to have my brother wait on me. I know it's his job and I have nothing but respect for a man making a respectable living. It's just a little strange to have my little brother, who used to fart on me and flick boogers at my shoes, serve me organic tea.

I offered my condolences to Mel and asked if we could talk about things. At first he gave me a 'who are you again' look, but he didn't say it. He nodded and sipped his tea.

"Marc has been here for a long time and he's having a hard time believing Mrs. Waterworth would harm herself."

Mel looked out ahead and nodded.

"Me too."

Tears filled his eyes.

"I know this is going to sound awful, but do you think it's possible that she didn't take her life?"

Mel looked hard into my eyes, then nodded.

"Who do you think could have done something like this?"

"Who could do something like this? I suppose any one of them, really." Mel shook his head and looked away. "Greed is a nasty thing. And not one of them doesn't have greed in their heart."

I nodded. "Which of them do you think could be capable of such a thing?"

"I don't know. Poppy was a great woman. Did you ever hear the story about how Poppy got her money?"

"Marc told me she won the lottery."

"Poppy was married before, to Angel's father. He passed when Angel was a boy, say twelve years ago or so. Several months later, Poppy's brother bought her a lottery ticket for her birthday," Mel sniffled. "She won. Poppy wasn't a greedy woman. She wanted to spread some of her wealth with her favorite charities and share it with her family. Lyle demanded half of the winnings since he bought the ticket. He didn't ask, he demanded. Poppy refused. She said she would share the money, but not half. That wasn't good enough for him. He sued her and lost. Poppy has tried to reconcile with Lyle many times since we've been married, but for him, it always comes down to the money."

"Sounds pretty nasty for him to sue his own sister over a gift he gave her," I said.

"Yeah, but it's not even the half of it when it comes to this family. Her sister is another nasty one. Rose has come to Poppy again and again about this business idea or that one. Poppy funded a few for Rose, but they would always fail. Rose doesn't know anything about running a business. In fact, two years ago, she opened a floral shop. As usual, it was near bankrupt. One night it went up in flames. The authorities determined the cause of the fire was arson. But they didn't have enough evidence to make any arrests."

"Strange coincidence," I responded.

"Yeah, it is. Rose received the insurance money and didn't bother Poppy for money for about ten months. Then, she came sniffing back around. Poppy refused her. She's asked a few more times, but Poppy finally put her foot down and told her no more money."

"I'm sorry to hear her family focused so much on her money and not the person Poppy was," I said.

"Me too, because she was a good woman. In many ways I think the money was a curse. I didn't know her before, but she didn't seem like the type to let money change her. Sure, she had this great-big house and all this land. She was a kind-hearted woman with principles. I truly loved her and still do."

"Thank you for your time Mr. Waterworth. I'll leave you be for now."

"Let me know if you have any other questions. Marc says you're the best private detective. I'm lucky to have you looking into my wife's passing," Mel stood and shook my hand. "Oh, and you might want to look into that son of Rose's. Boy's just like his mother. He's gotten tens of thousands out of Poppy over the years. Just yesterday afternoon, he asked for more. Poppy gave him the same speech she'd given his mother. He went on a tirade. He threw a vase across the room and told Poppy she'd regret being so stingy. You know, I don't want to believe she did this to herself, but I also don't want to believe that a member of her own family could do it either. I wish I could rewind back to last night. I wish it so badly."

I thanked Mel for his candor and for being so forthright with me.

Mel seems genuinely wounded by the loss of his wife.

It looks like I have my next three interviews to set up, but I'll need to talk to everyone. If Poppy was killed last night, it could be anyone.

[OPEN EVIDENCE ENVELOPE #2]

Went for a nice walk of the property with Marc a few minutes ago. The Waterworth estate is really stunning. The backyard isn't fenced and rolls on for about a half-acre before it comes upon the rocky shore. The stunning clear water lapping up on the volcanic-rock is the stuff dreams are made of.

Marc is still certain that Poppy was murdered. I explained my chat with Mel to Marc and explained that there are still many people to interview.

"So Mel thinks she was killed too?" Marc asked.

"Yes. He doesn't think she would harm herself, either. And, I'm beginning to think the same," I said.

"I've worked with Poppy for nearly half my life, Hudson. She's had some tribulations over the years. She was excited about the reunion. Having her family all come out and visit with her made her happy. Who could do something like this? And to such a wonderful lady?" Marc shook his head and looked out at the waves crashing against the rocks.

"I will get to the bottom of this. There is a small suspect pool here. And I'm quite sure none of them are professionals. If Poppy was murdered, I will find out who did it. You have my word."

"Thank you, Hudson."

"Tell me, what time did you go to sleep last night?" I asked.

"Probably around the same time as you. It had to be around midnight. We left at about quarter to twelve last night. I was bushwhacked. I didn't even shower. I stripped down and conked out."

"Did you see or hear anything to give you alarm at any time last night?" I asked.

"Nothing that stands out," Marc sighed. "Wait, I did see Lyle looking through Poppy's desk in the study. When he saw me, he said he was looking for a pen. The thing is, the pens are in a cup on top of the desk. I don't know if it helps, but it's all that comes to mind."

"That's great. Keep combing it through your mind and let me know if you recall anything else like that. I have a question. The suicide note, was that Poppy's stationary?"

"Yes, she has a tray of those little, square sheets in her desk," Marc nodded.

"It's odd, isn't it, that she wouldn't hand write the whole note? I mean, she would have had to type it up on the computer, then slip this tiny paper in the printer, then print it, and then sign the bottom. Wouldn't it have been easier to just write the note by hand? I mean the note was only a couple sentences."

"Hudson, that is very odd. I've received a few notes from Poppy on that very stationary over the years, and they've always been hand written."

Marc and I finished our tour of the property, then he left to attend to his duties.

If Poppy Waterworth was killed, then that means that there is a killer in that house. A person capable of taking another life is among us.

I finished my interviews with Poppy's brother and sister. Poppy's siblings weren't the easiest interviews I've ever had. They are very guarded, meaning, they may have something to hide. Part of it may be my fault. I am somewhat direct with my questions and not everyone takes too kindly to it. I find being direct catches people slightly off guard, and sometimes the answers they give aren't as important as their reactions.

I met with Lyle first. He is Poppy's older brother. We met in the library, the same place we all congregated last night after Poppy was found hanging in the hallway. I introduced myself and my profession. He agreed to answer a few of my questions.

"Do you think your sister ended her own life?" I asked.

"Well, it sure as hell looks like it. She was hanging from the rafters last night, now wasn't she?"

"Um...Why do you think she would do something like that?"

"How would I know? Yes, she was my sister, but we haven't talked in years, until she invited me to this reunion. I don't know what was going on in her life."

"I heard you two had a falling out over the lottery winnings," I said.

"Well, some people call me greedy and some call her a miser. I guess it's all in the perspective. She could have split all those millions with me. I bought the ticket that changed her life. She lived in squalor before the ticket, and now, look at all this. You know how much money she's given me?"

"I don't."

"Not one red cent!" He leaned in close. "Because I had the gumption to ask for half, we fought about it for years and I got zilch for my efforts."

"It sounds like this is still a hot issue for you," I said.

"Sure it is. My life could have been completely different. I'll never forgive that broad for all the trouble she's been through the years. She stopped being my sister a long time ago. I don't know, maybe she felt guilty for being such a penny-pincher when it came to her family and she couldn't bear it any longer. Maybe that's why she hung herself."

"Sounds a little harsh," I said.

"Maybe it is," he said with a shrug.

After a brief moment of silence, I asked, "You were in the study last night. Were you looking for something specific in Poppy's desk?"

He grinned, "I told your brother, I was looking for a pen."

"Marc told me that. But aren't the pens in a cup right on top of the desk?" I asked.

"I guess I didn't see them there." He shrugged, glaring at me.

I let the conversation sit there for a moment. I hoped that he would be more forthright with me. Something tells me, I could have waited until we were old men and he still wouldn't have talked.

"I only have one last question, where were you between midnight and 3am?"

Lyle stared at me for a long moment. He tried to size me up with that look. I could feel it.

"Asleep in my room, like everyone else. What are you getting at here? Do you think someone helped her or coerced her?"

"Right now, I'm only asking questions."

"On whose authority? You aren't the police. I agreed to your questions to be nice, but what are you trying to do here? You're trying to stir the pot. Find something, where there's nothing. Poppy killed herself. End of story. You shouldn't be poking around in our family business," He said, rising to his feet.

"Mel has given me his consent to look into her death," I said.

"Oh, Saint Mel," he spat out. "Did you ask Mel where he was last night? From where I stand he had the most to gain by her suicide. Him and that spoiled-rotten Angel. That name, Angel, what a laugh! More like a demon. I haven't seen a will or anything, but I imagine it all goes to them."

"Mel and Angel were on good terms with Poppy from what I hear," I said.

He chuckled.

"Well Mr. Private Investigator, Poppy told me last night she delayed Angel's inheritance because he's not the Angel he'd have people believe."

"I see. How long did she delay it and for what reason?" I asked. I'll admit, that caught me off guard.

"You're the detective, figure it out yourself," Lyle said, storming out of the library.

Sheesh! Not the friendliest guy around town.

Lyle is still clinging to his anger about the lottery winnings. That alone could be a motive for him to kill Poppy. It's too early to make assumptions; there are still many people for me to talk to.

I found Rose alone in the dining room eating a grilled cheese and a bowl of tomato soup. She looked so small in such a large room all alone. Extra large, oil paintings hung from the caramel-colored walls, combined with the dark wood floors, it gave the room a warm, welcoming feel.

I took a seat across the table from her. After offering my condolences and introducing myself, she agreed to my questions.

"What was your relationship like with Poppy?" I asked.

"I loved my sister, and she loved me."

"Why do you think she took her life?"

Rose began crying out loud. "I don't know."

She continued sobbing for a few moments. I gave her a time to collect herself. She blew her nose in her napkin and wiped her face with the other side.

"I heard she had cut you off financially," I mentioned.

"She's pretty much cut everyone off financially."

"I understand there was a questionable fire at your shop a while back."

She sniffed and straightened up, taking a more guarded posture.

"What are you getting at? Ancient history, buddy. No charges were filed. There was no proof I had anything to do with the fire," she said, taking a bite of her sandwich, without outright denying it.

"Can you think of anyone who might want to hurt Poppy or want her out of the way?"

"No, of course not! We are family. How could you even ask? Are you proposing someone did that to her? How absurd."

"Forgive me, I am simply trying to look at this from all angles. I only want to find out what happened."

"You were here. You know what happened. My sister killed herself last night. She hung herself in that very hallway," she said, pointing.

"But why? Why would she take her life? You were here last night. Did she seem suicidal to you? She certainly didn't seem it to me." I said, with more heat behind the words than I intended.

"I don't know why. You're right. She seemed happy at supper last night and afterward. We all have our demons Mr. Blackwell. Perhaps she kept hers to herself."

"One last question, and I mean no offense. Where were you last night between midnight and three?"

She lowered her voice, "After I saw Randall go into his room, I went out back. I was in the hot tub with...Chef Holloway. When I came in, I saw Poppy. I found her last night. Betty's room is closest. She was the first to come when I started screaming. Please don't say anything about me being with the chef. I don't want my son to find out about it. He already has a low opinion of me when it comes to men. I don't want my indiscretions to give Randall any more fuel than he already has."

"I will be discrete. You have my word."

After the interview with Rose, I have the distinct feeling she's not telling me the whole story. If she was still upset about being cut off, anger could be a motive.

I found Angel and Randall out at the pool. Angel's mother/ Randall's aunt was found dead less than twelve hours ago and these boys have decided to go for a swim.

"Hi there fellas, I'm Hudson Blackwell, Marc's brother. Do you gentlemen mind if I ask you a few questions?" I call out to them.

Randall shrugged. Angel stayed silent, glaring in my direction.

"How are you two holding up?" I asked.

"We're trying not to think about it," Randall said.

"I get it," I said. "I've been asked to look into things. I understand this is a difficult time, but I have a few questions. It's important, I ask them sooner, rather than later. With time, some of the details of the situation might fade."

"Are you a cop?" Angel asked, narrowing his eyes.

"No, I'm Marc's brother. We met last night. I'm a private investigator."

"Sure, what questions do you have?" Randall asked.

"I understand you and your aunt Poppy were involved in a disagreement yesterday. Could you tell me more about it?"

"I asked her for money. I should have known better. We got into an argument about it. That's all," Randall said.

"I heard you threw a vase across the room."

"I guess my temper got the best of me. She had so much, I mean, look at all this. My mom and I are getting evicted from our apartment again. We only needed $1200 to get us out, but Poppy said the well has dried up."

"I see. Did your mother ask her for money as well?"

Droplets of water landed on my arm as Angel swam away, purposefully kicking his feet.

"I think so. I mean, she was supposed to. We both were going to talk to Poppy separately. I don't know if she had a chance to ask."

"To you, did Poppy seem like the type of person who would take her own life?" I asked.

Randall shrugged. "I didn't know her well enough. I mean, she seemed fine after dinner, but who knows."

"Last night, where were you between midnight and three?"

"Sleeping in my room."

"My turn yet?" Angel asked, chewing on his blue-polished nails. He shook himself off like a dog, flinging droplets of water everywhere, including on me and Randall.

"Sure," I said, feeling mildly irritated. "Do you think your mother took her life?"

Angel stared at me for a moment as though he hadn't expected the question.

"I think it's obvious she did, Sherlock."

I bit my tongue. Sarcastic little brat.

"Did your mother seem depressed or upset? Is there any reason you can recall that might have led to her suicide?"

"Nah, not really. Most of the family didn't like her and she knew it. It might've upset her. This whole reunion thing was really important to her. Maybe seeing everyone again is what set her off."

"I heard your mother put off your inheritance. How did that happen?"

Angel sucked his cheeks in and his eyes turned cold. "I got caught smoking pot. She told me my priorities were askew. She deferred my inheritance until I turn 25, that's six years from now."

"It must have been disappointing," I said.

"I'll say, but life goes on right. There was nothing I could do about it."

"Where were you last night?"

"I hit the sack not long after Mom put Mel to bed," He shrugged.

It surprises me how cold Angel is acting. He lost his mother, possibly to suicide. I would have thought that of all the people here, he would be the most wounded by the loss of Poppy. I suppose he could be hiding his pain.

After interviewing Randall & Angel, I'm left with a hollow feeling. It seems this family is largely motivated by money. These boys are no different. I don't think they are revealing how they truly felt about the relationship they had with Poppy. Either one of them could have been her killer. I've seen people who've killed for less.

I still have to interview Chef Holloway and Betty Snyder. I think I'm going to head to the police station first to see if I can pry any information from them.

I ran into Chef Holloway this afternoon before I left for the police station. There wasn't any real information revealed, so I feel no need to dictate our conversation.

He confirmed meeting with Rose after the party, saying they enjoyed each other's company in the hot tub from about half past midnight until Rose found Poppy. He also asked me to keep it from Randall. I feel no need to reveal their transgressions to Randall, unless it's absolutely necessary. Holloway added that he and Rose discretely 'get together' whenever she visits. He didn't have much more to say. He seems to be genuinely upset by Poppy's passing. I saw no signs that he would do such a thing. He refused to discuss the rest of the family. He had nothing kind to say about them, so he'd rather not speak of them at all. I asked if he knew of anyone,

family or otherwise, that had reason to harm Poppy.
He said he couldn't imagine anyone harming her.

Chef Holloway and Rose could be covering for
each other, so I'm not going to rule them out. Unless
Holloway moonlights as an actor, I don't think he's
responsible. He seems to have cared for Poppy. I see
no motive for him to harm her, but there could be
more beneath the surface.

I met with Detective Richmond this afternoon. He's not too upset about me poking my nose into his investigation. I figured he'd give me the territorial cold shoulder, but this wasn't so much the case. As usual, I'm going to dictate our conversation. It helps me to remember the details.

Richmond agreed to meet with me at his desk at the station. His desk reminded me a little of mine at home, overflowing with case files and other clutter.

"What can I do for you Mr. Blackwell? Do you mind if I call you Hudson?" Richmond asked.

"Not at all, detective. I have spoken with Mrs. Waterworth's family, and some believe she wouldn't have killed herself. Is there any reason to believe that there might have been foul play?"

"I looked you up. A private detective in California. Well, this isn't California, so why don't you leave the investigating up to me."

"Of course," I said. "I understand. I was asked to look into it, that's all. And being that my brother and I are still staying on the estate grounds, I wouldn't want us to stay put if there is a murderer hanging about. I don't want to step on any toes, I only want to help, if I can."

The detective smirked before opening a file folder. "Well, those who believe that Mrs. Waterworth wouldn't have killed herself are right. The coroner has ruled the death a murder."

"I had a feeling."

I shook my head. I'm not sure how to feel about this. It's a relief to know that Poppy, a vibrant woman, didn't kill herself. But it also means that someone else took her life, which is very unsettling.

"As someone as well versed as yourself probably knows," Richmond began. "When someone hangs themselves a V-shaped bruise forms on the neck. In the case of Poppy, there was neck bruising, but in the shape of an inverted V."

"She was strangled?" I asked

I've handled strangling cases in the past. Not many, but enough to know this type of bruising comes from the shape of hands on the neck.

"It appears so. Then, her murderer strung her up to look like a suicide. Whoever did this was careless. They must have thought the coroner wouldn't figure it out. Clearly the work of an amateur. There is something else. There were black smudges on the rope she was hung with. I can't tell what it is. I have the lab testing it to determine the substance. My best guess is paint. We'll know more once the results come in," he said.

"Where did the rope come from?" I asked.

"Mr. Waterworth recognized it, when I took his statement, last night. He said it's been in the storage closet for years. Anyone would have had access to it, but not everyone would know that it was there."

"Does he know if the marks on the rope are new or if they've been there a while?" I questioned.

"He says he doesn't know."

"Were there any black smudges on Poppy's neck?" I asked.

"No, the substance was only found on the rope. She didn't have any black marks anywhere on her body."

"Poppy was a small woman, is it possible that a woman could have done this?" I asked.

"I suppose. Depends on the strength of the other woman."

"Do you have anyone you're looking at for this?" I asked.

"Do you Hudson?" Richmond raised an eyebrow. "Surely you must have a suspect or two in mind."

"Just about any of them. As far as I can tell they all wanted her money." I said with a frown. "Well, I've taken enough of your time detective. I'm sure I'll see you at the house soon enough for your follow-up questions."

"Yes, you will."

So it seems, Poppy Waterworth was strangled in a house full of people and made to look like she hanged herself. How could nobody have heard anything? How much time would it take to pull something like that off? Did the murderer kill her in the hallway or somewhere else? There are so many questions. I need to take a look inside the house again to gain more of a lay of the land. I think I'll sketch out a rough floor plan as a reference.

[OPEN EVIDENCE ENVELOPE #3]

Entry Date: March 5th 8pm

I just got back from dinner at a local brewing company. I am stuffed. I took my little brother out to dinner, on me. I thought it would be best to get away from the house. I had a few things I wanted to talk to him about, but didn't want eavesdroppers listening in. Now that Poppy's death has been confirmed as murder, we can't be too careful. If we touch a nerve with the killer, no telling what they might do to cover up their crime.

During our first round of lager, I explained what Detective Richmond shared with me.

"Nothing in the house has been painted lately. You say there was paint on the rope?" Marc asked.

"Richmond isn't sure. Some sort of substance is smeared all over the rope. It could be anything. The lab should be able to determine what it is," I said.

"I knew she didn't kill herself," Marc shook his head. "Have you told Mel yet?"

"No, you're the first to know kid. I figured since you put me on the case, I should let you know first. When I get back to the house, I'll let Mel know."

Marc ordered another round of lager, as our food arrived.

"Who do you think did this?" Marc asked in a whisper.

"I'm not sure yet. It seems like just about everyone in that house had a motive to murder Poppy. The question is, who actually would murder her. Her brother's still holding a hot grudge against her. Her sister is motivated by money. Her son's angry about his trust delay. I don't know about her cousin, but with the way things are going, I'm sure she has a motive too. I mean, there are many avenues here, but we'll figure it out."

"I know you will, you're the best private detective I know," Marc said, guzzling his beer.

"I'm the only private detective you know." I shook my head.

"True."

We ate until we couldn't eat anymore. The food was great and so was the beer. Spending time like this with my little brother is something we don't do often enough. I only wish, there hadn't been a murder on my trip.

The stuff on that rope is bothering me. It was only on the rope...Could it have been something that happened ages ago, or could it have been left by the murderer?

I was finally able to track down Betty Snyder. All day I've been trying to pin down this lady. I met with her about an hour ago in the parlor.

"You're a hard lady to track down, been looking to talk to you all day," I said.

"I've been out," she replied, lighting a cigarette. "I had some things to take care of."

"I understand, it's a difficult time right now and there's much to be done. I spoke to the detective a while ago and he has ruled Poppy's death a murder."

"A murder?" Betty whispered, lowering her head and narrowing her eyes.

"Based on the bruising on her neck, it looks like Poppy was strangled."

"Strangled?" Betty gasped. "Are you saying that someone in this house strangled Poppy, then made it look like she killed herself? What about the note?" She whispered, looking over her shoulder.

"The killer must have planted it, hoping it would be an open and shut case. Based on the bruising, there's no way she could have hanged herself," I said.

"Who do you think did it?" She whispered so softly, I could hardly make it out.

"Well, that's a tough one. Based on the conversations I've had, there's a lot of bad blood. Speaking of, I understand you and Mrs. Waterworth were at odds too?"

"Just what are you saying? You think I could do something like this?" She stood from her chair, her long, dark hair draped around her shoulders.

"I'm only asking questions. Your insight could help to find Poppy's killer. Please, I meant no offense."

Betty sat down, but she was definitely ruffled.

"I have nothing to hide. I was in my room last night. I was on my laptop, video chatting with my boyfriend until I heard the screaming. Phil, my boyfriend, heard the screams too, as a matter of fact. And I'll tell you, it was a mood killer, if you get what I mean. I gave my laptop to the cop who called earlier. He's looking into my laptop and the video records."

"Was it Detective Richmond, you gave the laptop to? When was he here?"

"He called a couple hours ago. He asked again about where I was at the time of Poppy's death. I volunteered my laptop for him to check. That's where I was earlier. I stopped by the police station to drop it off. He didn't mention anything about a murder, but maybe it was a tactic. I figured that he wanted to make sure no one helped her. Plus, it gave me an opportunity to make a dinner date tomorrow with the cop who interviewed me last night."

"I see. Don't you have a boyfriend?" I asked.

"Mr. Blackwell, what he doesn't know...Besides, you can't possibly think that a woman like me could be shackled to one man," she whispered, biting her lip.

I admit it, I blushed. I'm used to being the one to catch others off guard, but Betty turned the tables on me. I cleared my throat and went back to my questions.

"Tell me about your relationship with Poppy," I asked.

She sighed.

"It could have been better. I guess, in looking at it now, we all kind of looked at her as our cash cow. I gamble. I have debt on the books. I always owe on a marker or two. Poppy bailed me out more times than I'd like to admit. I was going to ask for money to pay off my bookie this time too, but I didn't have a chance. She wouldn't have helped me though. Last time, she said she wouldn't do it again."

"Have you thought about getting help, I mean with the gambling?" I asked.

"Mr. Blackwell, there's no help for me."

"The postcard Poppy sent you for the reunion was found at the scene. How do you suppose it got there?" I asked.

"I had it with me during the get together, it must have fallen out of my handbag at some point. I don't know why it was there. Perhaps Poppy found it and had it with her at the time of...well...you know," she said.

"Why do you think someone would do this to Poppy? I mean what would they get out of it?" I asked.

"Why else, Mr. Blackwell? It has to be for the money. I'd look closer at her immediate family. She had Mel sign a prenup before they were married. And that son of hers... He's in a class of his own. Poppy was trying to teach him responsibility, but that self-entitled brat didn't get it. She was going to put him out, you know."

I did a double take, "Who? Angel?"

"Yup. She told him he needed to get a job and start paying his way. He didn't. She gave him three months to move out on his own and learn some real-life skills. That way, when he comes into his trust fund, he might handle it better," she shrugged.

"Mel seemed happy with Poppy. Why do you think he'd do something like this? I mean, he still had access to the money while married to her?"

"I don't know if Mel did it or not," she shook her head. "What if he wanted to play the field?"

"Or what if he already found someone else?" I questioned.

"Exactly." She smiled.

"Do you think he's the foolin' around type?" I asked.

"He's a man, now isn't he?" Betty narrowed her eyes.

I didn't take offense to her comment though part of me feels like she intended to offend me.

"Thank you for your time Betty. Oh, and have you seen Mel?"

"Oh, the pleasure was all mine, Mr. Blackwell. Mel said he was heading to bed early at about eight or so. Haven't seen him since."

In looking back at our conversation, I have the feeling that Betty is the type of woman that'd chew a man up and spit him out when she's done with him. There is something about that lady that draws me to her and terrifies me at the same time. I fully believe she's capable of murder, but whether she murdered Poppy or not, it's too early to tell. I'll have to check with Detective Richmond to see if her alibi checks out.

It looks like I'll have to wait until morning to talk to Mel. I hope he wakes up early.

I met with Mel, this morning. I like the guy, but I had to ask him the same questions as everyone else. Yesterday, he was still pretty broken when I met with him. Today, he was a little better.

We met in the lounge. We sat looking out floor to ceiling windows with a view of the pool and spa in the back yard. Marc brought us a tray of fruit and a coffee carafe with all the fixings. After we'd poured our cups, and a few minutes of small talk, I dove right in to my questions.

"Mel, I have to ask," I began. "Where were you, the night it happened?"

Mel nodded. "Passed out I guess. I remember Poppy helping me to the room, but after that, nothing. Until I heard the screaming. I turned to Poppy's side of the bed and she was gone. Then I thought it was her screaming. I scrambled out of bed to get to her. When I reached the hallway—"

Mel took a deep breath and looked down.

I stayed silent, allowing him time to collect himself.

"I saw her at the end of the hall. I wasn't sure if it was her or not. The farther down the hall I went, the more I realized it was her. Poppy. The love of my life. I couldn't imagine why she would do something like that to herself."

"Mel, I spoke to the detective. He said, based on the shape of the bruising on her neck, she didn't do that to herself," I said.

Mel stared at me, before narrowing his eyes. "What exactly are you saying?"

"According to the coroner's report, she was...strangled."

Mel leapt to his feet. He paced a few times before turning back to me. "Someone, in this house, murdered her? I knew you were looking into it, but it seemed impossible. It also seemed impossible that she would hurt herself. Who did this?"

"I'm looking into it and so is the detective. He'll be by soon enough. I understand that Poppy was going to force Angel to move out?"

"No! Someone in this house killed my wife!"

"Mel, please calm down. We're going to find out who did this, I promise."

He paced a few more times, seething. He finally stopped. He stood in place with his chest heaving. After about a minute, he nodded.

"I'm sorry. I...uh...it's overhwhelming. What was your question?" Mel asked.

"No need to apologize. I get it. Had Poppy asked Angel to move out?"

Mel sighed and took his seat. "Yeah. She didn't think he was responsible at all. He got into some trouble, so Poppy deferred his trust. He got into more trouble, so she cut him off financially. Then he started selling drugs. Poppy gave him three months to move out. She wasn't about to give a troubled young man a boatload of money. She wanted to see some responsibility out of him, but he failed every time."

"How much time did he have left?" I asked.

"Three weeks. Honestly, the kid's a screw-up. I don't think he has what it takes to do something like this."

"Then who do you think could do something like this?" I asked.

"Lyle. I think all his pent up anger and jealousy is as vivid today as it was a decade ago. And, he's got a temper. All Poppy wanted to do was to get everyone back together to remember the old times and make new memories. She hoped her family could look past the money and see her again. No one could do it. Not one of them could see her for the wonderful woman she was. And now, she's gone. I hope it eats each and every one of them up inside."

A knock on the open lounge door echoed through the space.

"Knock, knock," Detective Richmond called out. "I hope I'm not interrupting."

"Come in detective," Mel said.

"Thank you Mr. Waterworth. We met the other night, I'm Detective Richmond."

"Yes, yes, I remember. And you know Hudson Blackwell," Mel stood up to greet Richmond.

"Yes, I take it that Mr. Blackwell shared with you the coroner's findings."

"He just told me."

"Hudson, would you mind giving me a few minutes to speak to Mr. Waterworth?"

"I would like him to stay," Mel shrugged.

"Hudson," Richmond said, nodding toward the door.

"I'd like to stay," I said.

"Okay, here's the deal, may I call you Mel?" Richmond grinned, cocking his head in annoyance.

Mel nodded slowly.

"Either Mel and I can conduct our interview here without your presence, Hudson. Or Mel and I can take a ride to the station."

"I'll wait for you in the study," I said.

"That's better," Richmond said.

This detective is working my nerves. I don't like this, not at all.

"Detective, quick question. Betty said you were checking her laptop to verify her alibi. Have you had a chance to check on it?"

"Yes Hudson. Our tech analyst looked into Betty's video chatting claim and it all checked out. She was video chatting with her boyfriend in Keyes, California during the time window."

"Thank you detective," I said, leaving the lounge.

Just when I thought I'd gotten somewhere with Richmond, he pulls this? What is the problem with me sitting in on the interview? I have a strange feeling about this, I hope it's only a feeling and not something that will come into fruition.

Upon arriving in the study, I find it empty. I sit behind a desk that must have belonged to Poppy. The desk is decorated with flowers and light colors. I smooth my hands across the lacquered wood desk top as if trying to channel her spirit to ask who'd done this to her. I notice the corner of a paper sticking out of the top, right drawer. I look around, but no one is there to see me.

I gently pull open the drawer and glance at the page. It's an email addressed to Poppy. The contents of this email could be motive for murder.

As if on cue, Betty strolls into the study. She gives me a sideways smile.

"Betty, were you aware that your bookie sent this email to your cousin?"

"No, hi Betty, you're looking stunning today? Just right in with the questions, huh?" She shrugged. "Yes. I knew about the email."

"Did Poppy discuss it with you? She printed it out, which means she wanted to show it to someone. I'm guessing that someone was you."

Betty went stone-faced, then looked the other way. She sighed, before making eye contact.

"She showed me the email. I told her I didn't want her stinking money. I could figure it out for myself. She offered to give me the money if I went into a rehab facility for gamblers. I told her to blow it out her nose. We quarreled, but nothing out of hand. That is actually when she got the post card from me. I sort of, flung it at her after the rehab comment.

Afterward, I went to my room and vented to my boyfriend through video chat. I didn't mention it earlier, or to the cops because I didn't want them or you to know we argued."

"What time was all this?"

"I started the video chat at 11:55pm. So I last saw her maybe three-five minutes prior. Look, I'm no killer, Hudson. I don't know who did this, but it wasn't me."

[OPEN EVIDENCE ENVELOPE #4]

I've waited nearly an hour for the interview with Detective Richmond and Mel Waterworth to wrap up and it still hasn't.

After my conversation with Betty, I decided to take another walk around the place, thinking I might spot some sort of clue or something that could point this investigation in the right direction.

I heard a knock on the front door, followed by Angel calling out, "Pizza's here."

I followed my nose to the dining room. Angel, Randall, and Rose were already there, along with the pizza delivery guy.

"Okay, I need a signature on the screen," the pizza guy announced.

"I'll get the plates," Angel announced. "Go ahead and sign for it Randall."

Randall took a contraption from the delivery driver and signed on a screen with an attached stylus. The driver then, printed out a receipt and handed it to Randall.

"Thanks! Enjoy the pizza," the driver said, heading out the front door.

Lyle came into the dining room with Betty not far behind. I began to grow concerned with how long things were taking between Mel and the detective.

Randall took the first slice. Angel stood behind him, biting his purple nails.

A new color every day.

The boys plopped down in the chairs at the end of the table and began eating their pizza.

Betty sashayed up to the stack plates. I don't know why she's trying to act sexy, everyone here is family, except me. And it certainly couldn't be for my benefit.

"Ugh," Betty sighed. "I smudged my polish."

A bright pink streak stained the rim of her plate. Part of me thought that served her right for being so vain.

"Maybe you should let your nails dry before pigging out on pizza. You know you could stand to miss a few meals," Lyle snickered.

"Blow it out your nose, Lyle. These are called curves, but I don't suppose you know much about that. You probably have to pay to see curves like this up close," she snapped back.

"Keep eating Betty and those curves are going to turn into a fat ass," Lyle responded.

"Can we keep it civil?" Rose butted in. "Seriously, you two?"

Then, it struck a chord with me. I figured something out in that moment, not the whole puzzle, but a piece of it.

I finished my slice of pizza while scrutinizing the others. I almost have this case in the bag, but I'm still missing something. I need to think on it for a couple minutes.

It was about 11:30am when Marc came in to clear the dining room of the used plates and pizza boxes. I proceeded to help him. I gathered the boxes and noticed the receipt on the table. I snatched it up and went to the kitchen. I placed the boxes on the counter and tossed the receipt in the trash. I made it about four steps before heading back to the trash can. I pulled out the receipt and examined it closely.

Detective Richmond finally emerged from the lounge with Mel Waterworth in handcuffs.

"What's this all about?" Rose asked as the men walked past the dining room toward the front door.

"You should know," Richmond said.

"Detective. What's happening?" I asked.

"I am arresting Melvin Waterworth for suspicion of murder."

"On account of what evidence?" Betty inquired.

"You mean aside from the fact that he knew where the rope was stored, has no one to corroborate his flimsy alibi and he has the strength and size to commit a murder like this and easily set up the scene to look like a suicide? Well, how about this, I believe Mel has been having an affair with Rose Harbone. There is a prenuptial agreement with a stipulation for cheating. I have phone records showing quite a few, late-night calls over the last few weeks between you two. Mel killed Poppy so she wouldn't find out and he'd get to keep all this," Richmond announced.

"What an absurdity!" Rose threw her hands up. "There have been no phone calls and no affair with Mel, I assure you."

"Detective, those calls could have been from Poppy," I said.

"There weren't any late-night calls. Not from Mel and not from Poppy," Rose said. "Other than a single call from Poppy inviting me to the reunion, I haven't heard either one of their voices in years. Check your records again, detective. Neither one of them called my house."

"Detective, I have a theory that I think might blow this case wide open. If you'll remove the cuffs from Mel for just long enough for me to explain it to you. I'm sure you want to hear what I have to say," I told Richmond.

Richmond chuckled. "Fine, I'll play along, but the cuffs stay on."

Richmond and Mel followed me to the hall.

"Look, I know what I have on Mel is circumstantial, but it's enough to make an arrest and hold him. Mel is the most likely suspect, he had the most to gain," Richmond said. "I can't leave him in this house to cover up any more evidence than he may have already. Tell me your theory. Let's get on with it."

I shook my head. I've never met someone so eager to make an arrest on so little.

"There have been a few things that have been nagging at me. I think in order to find out who killed Poppy Waterworth, we have to follow the clues."

[OPEN EVIDENCE ENVELOPE #5]

Note from Caretaker:

Pardon the Interruption.

It appears that this is where Mr. Hudson Blackwell thinks he's solved the case. If you have been following along and reviewing the clues, this would be the part in this adventure that you make your attempt at solving the case.

Based on Mr. Blackwell's journal notes and the clues he gathered, do you have a prediction of who murdered Poppy Waterworth and why? If you do, then read on to Mr. Blackwell's reveal. If you do not, you can take time to review the evidence and the clues before proceeding.

Please note, that the solution to this crime will be revealed in the next section.

I collected my file of clues on the case and this journal and asked that the detective and the family follow me to where Poppy was found, outside the game room. Once we arrived, I pulled out the photo of the rope.

"You see, this has been bothering me the whole time, up until Betty came to lunch. She smudged her hot pink polish on her plate," I said.

"What does that have to do with the rope?" Betty asked.

"Everything," I said. "You see, these black smudges on the rope? I am sure that they are black nail polish. I'm sure the police lab can confirm that."

"Yes, actually. They are testing the substance as we speak, but the results won't be in until the end of the week," Richmond said.

"Fine," Lyle chimed in. "But nobody here is wearing black nail polish."

"That's true, today. But on the night of Poppy's murder, someone was wearing black nail polish," I said.

I paused to let the killer come forward, but it wouldn't be that easy.

"Angel, I noticed that your nails had been painted black on the night of the party. They were chipped because you were biting your nails for most of the night. I suspect you repainted them as you were waiting to make your move, but you didn't let them dry completely before handling the rope. The next day, in the pool, I noticed your nails were painted metallic blue. Now, they are purple. For someone who bites their nails as much as you do, I'm willing to bet there is DNA evidence mixed in with the polish. It's only a matter of waiting on the lab."

"You're wrong, my nails weren't black. You guys can't prove it," Angel said.

"I don't need to," Richmond said. "The evidence will do all the proving for us. You might have thought you were smart enough to outsmart the police, but you aren't. And you sure aren't smarter that the lab. Tell us son, why did you do this to your mother?"

"Don't call me son. My father is dead. My mother too. I'm nobody's son anymore," Angel sucked in his cheeks and shook his head. "That cheapskate wouldn't give me my trust. I had plans, you know. I've known what I would do with the money since I was fifteen. So she was going to make me wait even longer? Then she kicks me out? I don't think so. I just wanted my piece of the money so I could go out and live my own life. I almost got it too. With her out of the way my trust would have diverted to me."

"You selfish little bastard!" Mel shouted. "How could you do such a thing to the person who loved you most in this world? She was your mother! You stupid, stupid little boy."

Tears fell from Mel's eyes as he struggled to keep himself from charging at Angel.

"I've heard enough. You're under arrest Angel," Richmond announced. He uncuffed Mel and slipped the handcuffs on Angel. After reading him the Miranda rights, Richmond proceeded down the hall toward the door.

"Detective Richmond, there's more that I'm sure you'd like to hear," I call after him.

"We got the guy Hudson, there is nothing else."

"I promise, you'll want to hear this next part," I said. "You see, Angel wasn't alone in the plot to kill Poppy."

"Are you saying someone helped that monster kill my wife?" Mel growled.

"There weren't any nail polish smudges on Poppy's neck. The coroner determined that she was strangled. If Angel had done it, he would have left similar smudges on her skin. I actually believe that Angel helped someone else kill Poppy."

"It was you wasn't it?" Lyle said, glaring at Mel.

"Of course not!" Mel shouted. "How could you even suggest—"

"No, it was not Mel," I jump in. "But it explains the calls that you were referring to a few moments ago, detective. Those calls were between Angel and Randall."

Randall shrunk back to the wall behind him.

"Don't you drag my son through the mud," Rose wagged her finger at me.

"You see, Rose knew nothing of the calls. That's because they were between Angel and Randall. After I figured out the nail polish smudges, I knew there had to be a second suspect. It wasn't until I took a second look at this pizza receipt that I knew it was Randall."

"This is absurd! How could a pizza receipt point to my son?" Rose questioned.

"You see, the boys had the forethought to type up Poppy's suicide note on her stationary. They forgot something important though, to sign it. It surely must have been an afterthought. We know from the postcard that Poppy sent Betty that the signature on the suicide note is not her handwriting. Randall signed the note. The handwriting matches his signature on the pizza receipt."

"I knew we should have left the note unsigned," Randall said, looking to Angel.

"Not another word," Rose commanded.

"Why Mom? Ashamed at what you've raised? Yeah, I killed Poppy in the game room. Then me and Angel hoisted her up and left the note. Angel promised to give me two million of his trust money and I saw it as my way out of the life that I have. And a way to get away from you, living hand to mouth."

Detective Richmond arrested both young men on first degree murder charges. He thinks that they may have concocted the scheme long before the reunion. I don't disagree with him.

Mel thanked me for finding justice for his wife. The rest of the family was cordial. Marc asked me to stay an extra day for some real vacation time, but I had to go. He was relieved that I was able to get to the bottom of what happened to Poppy. Marc isn't sure if he's going to stay on at the waterworth estate. I told him to put some thought into what would make him happy.

I think in my own life, I should heed that advice.

Entry Date: March 14th

I received a call from Marc. He decided to resign. Apparently, Poppy Waterworth left almost her entire estate to her husband. It looks like Poppy included Marc in her will. She left him a sum of money. Marc wouldn't tell me on the phone. He's sending me a care package and is going to slip in a copy of the will.

I just hope that money doesn't go to his head. Or attract the looneys.

[OPEN ENVELOPE #6]

CASE

SOLVED

51926834R00063

Made in the USA
San Bernardino, CA
06 August 2017